CUMBRIA LIBRARIES

3 8003 04775

KT-178-007

Prais

'Will make you laugh out loud, cringe and snigger, all at the same time'
LoveReading4Kids

'Very funny and cheeky'
—Booktictac, Guardian Online Review

Waterstones Children's Book Prize Shortlistee!

'I LAUGHED SO MUCH, I THOUGHT THAT I WAS GOING TO BURST!'
Finbar, aged 9

'The review of the eight year old boy in our house... "Can I keep it to give to a friend?" Best recommendation you can get' - Observer

'HUGELY ENJOYABLE, SURREAL CHAOS'
-Guardian

I am still not a Loser
WINNER of
The Roald Dahl
FUNNY PRIZE
2013

First published in Great Britain 2013
by Jelly Pie, an imprint of Egmont UK Ltd
The Yellow Building, 1 Nicholas Road, London W11 4AN

Text and illustration copyright © Jim Smith 2013
The moral rights of the author-illustrator have been asserted.

ISBN 978 1 4052 6032 9

barryloser.com

jellypiecentral.co.uk

A CIP catalogue record for this title is available from the British Library

Printed and bound in Great Britain by the CPI Group

49954/8

All rights reserved. No part of this publication may be reproduced,
stored in a retrieval system, or transmitted, in any form or by any means,
electronic, mechanical, photocopying, recording or otherwise, without the
prior permission of the publisher and copyright owner.

Stay safe online. Any website addresses listed in this book are correct at the time of going
to print. However, Egmont is not responsible for content hosted by third parties. Please be
aware that online content can be subject to change and websites can contain content that
is unsuitable for children. We advise that all children are supervised when using the internet.

MIX
Paper
FSC   FSC® C018306

"still" not I am a Loser

starring Noseypoos!

Barry Loser

Commas put in by Jim Smith

Hover-poos

You know when someone's horrible to you in a dream and you wake up really annoyed with them? That's what happened to me with my best friend Bunky.

me

Bunky

In the dream I was my favourite TV character, **Future Ratboy**, and Bunky was his annoying sidekick Not Bird.

Future Ratbarry (me)

Not Bird/ Bunky

extra-thick granny carpet

RB

We were in the mayor's office, which looked exactly like my granny's house.

'You're the only ones who can save us from the hoverpoos!' said the mayor, who was played by my teacher, Mr Hodgepodge.

Mayor Hodgepodge

weird dream things

Hoverpoos were the invention of Professor Smugly, who in the dream was Gordon Smugly from our class at school.

smug

ugly

Gordon Smugly has the most perfect name for himself ever in the history of having a name, because he looks like a Gordon and is smug and ugly.

Professor Smugly had given all the dogs in town his hoverpoo potion so that now, instead of their poos landing splat on the ground, they hovered ten centimetres above it.

'They're everywhere!' said the mayor, screaming as a hoverpoo floated up and bumped into his sock.

It was about the same size as Not Bird (Bunky) and the same colour (brown) and also floated (like birds can).

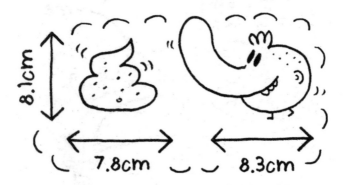

'Don't worry, Mayor Hodgepodge, we'll stop Professor Smugly!' I said, and I looked at his face to see if he was impressed, but he was too busy screaming and kicking at the hoverpoo to notice.

Because it was a dream, all of a sudden we were in Professor Smugly's laboratory and I'd turned myself into a fly, and was sitting on Not Bird's beak.

'What's all this craziness about?' said Professor Smugly, holding a test tube with brown bubbling potion in it.

'Ooh, can I have a sip?' said Not Bird, flying over to the test tube.

He perched on the edge and dipped his beak in. 'Ahhhhhhh,' he said, and he turned straight into a hoverpoo.

'Hmmm . . . a talking hoverpoo. That could be useful,' said Professor Smugly, flicking me off Not Bird's head.

'Not Bird, how do you fancy being my right-hand man?' he said.
'Or should I say right-hand poo?'

'But Bunky's MY right-hand poo!'
I screamed, but because I was a fly
it came out as a whisper.

'Barrrrr-yyyyy, you'll be late for
schooo-oooll!' my mum shouted up the
stairs, and I woke up, not a fly any
more, and late for school.

Grandpa Hodge-podge

'Thanks for making me late!' said Bunky at the top of my road where he waits for me in the morning, and he wasn't being sarcastic either.

'Oh I'm SOOOO sorry, what, do you have to meet Professor Smugly or something?' I said, in full **Future Ratboy** sarcastic mode.

'Who's Professor Smugly?' said Bunky, picking his nose and eating it for breakfast.

'Don't pretend you don't know, HOVERPOO,' I said, and I gave him my evil stare.

'What's a hoverpoo?' said Bunky, and he scrunched himself up into a poo shape and pretended to hover around, doing blowoffs, and I crumpled to the floor like a deckchair being folded up, weeing myself with laughter.

The walk to school takes us past Granny Harumpadunk's house, which I've been trying to avoid ever since she started going out with my teacher, Mr Hodgepodge.

I usually manage to sneak past just before they have their disgusting morning kiss at the front gate, but because we were late, Bunky and me got there the exact millisecond their dried-up old lips started snogging.

Granny Harump-adunk

Mr Hodge-podge

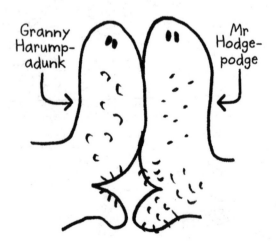

I closed my eyes to stop myself being sick and tried to tiptoe past, but what with Bunky doing his hoverpoo impression and me tripping over Granny's empty milk bottles, and Mr Hodgepodge kissing Granny with his eyes open anyway, it didn't really work.

titter

honk

'Ooh, Hodge, you can give Barry and Blinky a lift!' said Granny, so that was how we ended up in Mr Hodgepodge's car.

'Hodge' is Granny Harumpadunk's nickname for Mr Hodgepodge, who's the happiest person in the whole wide world amen now that he's going out with her.

'Isn't it the most incredibly beautiful day!' he said, in his new woolly jumper that matches Granny's.

He was squeezing into the front seat of his car, all wheezing and blowing off, and I looked at Bunky's eyes in the rear-view mirror and did a little snortle.

I was a bit annoyed that we were getting a lift with Mr Hodgepodge, mainly because of how embarrassing it was, but also because I couldn't go into Three Thumb Rita's.

third
thumb

Three Thumb Rita's is the tiny sweet shop halfway between my house and school. It's owned by Rita, who has an extra thumb on one of her hands, which sounds disgusting but actually isn't once you've seen it every day for a million years.

She even sells little Thumb Sweets,
which are my complete and utter
favourites.

'Mooooooooorrrrrrnnnnniiiinnnnngggggg Riiiitttttaaaaa!' I screamed out of the car as we zoomed past, because I didn't want her to think I'd started going to another sweet shop because of her third thumb or something.

I don't think she heard or saw me though.

'There's Barry and Bunky with their new grandad!' shouted Darren Darrenofski as we drove through the front gates at school, Mr Hodgepodge blowing off to the song on the radio.

Anton's cuddly Future Ratboy

← Anton

'I'm not with them!' shouted Bunky out of the window as we parked, and he got out and zoomed off like a talking hoverpoo, not that it mattered because his first lesson was with me and Mr Hodgepodge anyway.

Jealous little hairs

'I thought we could do something really fun today!' Mr Hodgepodge said once we'd all sat down at our desks. 'As you know, my new girlfriend is Barry Loser's granny, and this lesson is all about something she said last night!'

Everyone laughed, and I imagined
Mr Hodgepodge accidentally treading
on a couple of hoverpoos and floating
off into the sunset, never to be seen
again.

The End

'Well, we were watching TV, and
there was an advert for one of these
mobile phone thingymajigs,' he said.

Darren Darrenofski was scraping the back of my neck with his ruler. I turned round and he did a little burp and blew it into my face.

swish

'Barry's granny was amazed,' said Mr Hodgepodge. ' "Telephones you can carry around?" she said, "Ooh, what will they think of next!" '

ring ring

Granny's phone (Ethel calling)

If I wasn't Barry Loser and
Mr Hodgepodge wasn't going out
with Granny Harumpadunk, I would've
laughed along with the rest of the class
at his impression of an old granny.

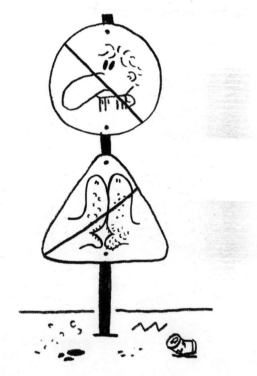

But I am. And he is. So I didn't.

'So today's lesson is called What Will They Think of Next!' Mr Hodgepodge said and he pointed at me.

'Barry, what do you think they'll think of next?'

scrape

'Ooh, Barry first, what a surprise,' said
Tracy Pilchard, and her, Donnatella
and Sharonella all started giggling, not
that I cared, because this was exactly
the kind of lesson I'm completely
brilliant and amazing at.

'I was thinking it'd be keel if when you thought of something, it popped up in a bubble above your head like in cartoons,' I said, because that was what happened in a **Future Ratboy** episode once.

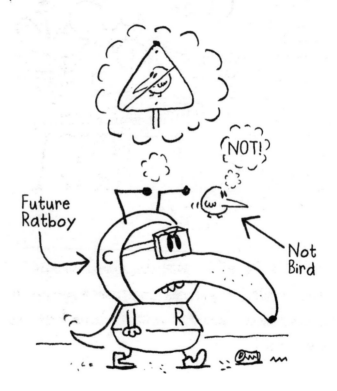

twist

Fay Snoggles's
rubber

'What's "keel"?' said Jocelyn Twiggs,
and I rolled my eyes because everyone
knows that 'keel' is how **Future Ratboy**
says 'cool'.

I looked at Mr Hodgepodge to see if he was impressed with my keel idea, but he wasn't even listening.

'What about you, Tracy?' he said after the length of a whole episode of **Future Ratboy**.

He was staring at a photo of Granny he had on his desk.

'I reckon they should make more jewellery,' said Tracy, and Donnatella and Sharonella both agreed, even though they all had about five hundred bits of jewellery on already.

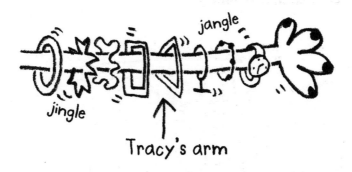

jangle

jingle

Tracy's arm

'Gordon?' said Mr Hodgepodge, and I looked over at Gordon Smugly for the first time since my dream. He was sitting at the back of the classroom, playing on his new phone.

'Thank you, Mr Hodgepodge,' he said, looking up from his game. 'Well now, there has been something bothering me for a while, and I suppose this is as good a time as any to make it known, publicly, so to speak,' he carried on, and I rolled my eyes so much that it made me feel dizzy.

'I think they should make a
Future Ratboy film,' he said, and I felt
all the little hairs everywhere on my
entire body stand up on end.

I think my little hairs are even bigger
fans of **Future Ratboy** than I am,
because whenever anyone else
mentions him they get instantly
jealous.

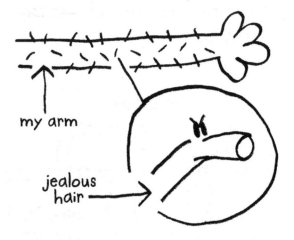

my arm

jealous
hair

'Yeeaa-aaah!' said everybody, because
it was actually a really good idea.
A **Future Ratboy** film would be keel
times a million.

'What's all this **Future Ratboy** business?' asked Mr Hodgepodge, looking up from the photo. I was going to stand up and explain, seeing as I'm **Future Ratboy's** number-one fan, but I was still a bit dizzy from my eye roll so I just sat there like a loser.

eye roll

Brian's burger

Brian's burgers

'**Future Ratboy** is the keelest TV show in the whole wide world ever!' said Bunky, copying what I was going to say.

wobble

He looked at Gordon and did a little snortle, but only because he wanted a go on Gordon's phone.

'Well, I can see that Bunky and Gordon are quite the experts on Future Ratman!' said Mr Hodgepodge, and I could feel all my clothes being pushed away from my skin by my jealous little hairs.

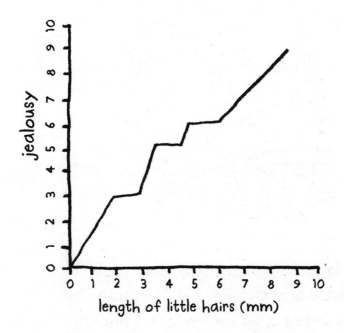

length of little hairs (mm)

Feeko's Super- market

The next day was Saturday, except
I call it 'Sat', because I've started
shortening my words to save time
for keeler stuff.

Sat is my favourite day because all me and Bunky do for the whole of it is play it completely and utterly keel. Like last Sat, when we went to the ginormous new Feeko's Supermarket in town.

'Let's go to Feeko's again!' I said when I came downstairs for breakfast and found Bunky in the living room watching TV as usual.

My dad was watching TV too, but through the window from the garden, which is where he usually is for the whole of HIS Sat.

'Do we have to do that again?' said Bunky, doing his loser face.

'Do you want me to send you home?' I said, and he stopped doing his loser face and started doing his worried one, because I sent him home last week for not saying I was his brilliant and amazing leader, and only let him back once he'd apologised.

Going to Feeko's Supermarket has been my favourite thing to do since I saw the episode of **Future Ratboy** where he went into one and bought a hoverpizza.

'Wow, look Bunky, they've got that
new washing powder from the advert
on TV!' I said as we walked into
Feeko's, except I was running a bit,
because I was so excited.

'Ooh, washing powder, excuse me while I wee myself,' said Bunky, trying to be sarcastic but just coming across as annoying.

'Salute it NOW!' I ordered, and Bunky did his loser face, then a tiny little salute. Saluting stuff is my new favourite thing to do, by the way.

A mum walked past with her kids and I rolled my eyes to her like mums do to each other, because in a way Bunky is like my child who I have to teach what is keel and what isn't.

As we walked up to the Ready Meals section to see if they'd started selling hoverpizzas yet, I sensed something familiar and annoying to my right.

Looking down the Household Goods aisle, I saw Darren Darrenofski with his mum, who I recognised because she looked just like him except with permed hair and a dress on.

Darren had wrapped himself in a whole tube of cling film and was caterpillaring along the floor like one of those insects with loads of legs that turn into butterflies that I can never remember the name of.

Darren's mum was watching him all calmly, but in the way mums look just before they start shouting. I leaned against a massive pyramid of toilet rolls and got myself cozy for watching Darren being told off.

53

I was just about to order Bunky to salute Darren's going-to-get-told-off-ness when he started dancing around all Bunkily and tapping me on the shoulder and shouting 'Salute! Salute! Salute! Salute!'

'There IS such a thing as over-saluting, Bunky,' I said, turning round to look, then immediately realised that there wasn't. 'SA-LUUUUUUUTE!' I screamed, and started running towards the thing I was saluting.

Cola Flavour Not Birds

You know how I said Three Thumb Rita's
Thumb Sweets were my favourites?
That was before I saw Feeko's
Cola Flavour Not Birds.

'Salute!' I shouted in Bunky's ear as I grabbed a packet, and he did a massive salute, twirling his hand around before it got to his forehead, which means that what you're saluting is extra keel.

keelest
front
of pack
ever

keelest
back
of pack
ever

We ran up to the checkout, blowing off with excitement, and bought five packets each, me buying six so that I had one more than Bunky.

It was a self-checkout, which meant there wasn't anyone serving you, so we beeped the packets through ourselves, the robot voice saying, 'Colar. Flavar. Not. Birdz,' eleven times.

Granny   Hodge

'Barry!' I heard from behind me, in a loserish non-self-checkout-robot voice. I turned round and saw Granny Harumpadunk and Mr Hodgepodge standing behind two completely full-up trolleys.

'I'm. Outta. Here,' said Bunky in his rubbish self-checkout robot voice, and he zoomed off at Super Not Bird speed, probably because he didn't want anyone thinking Mr Hodgepodge was his grandad, and I don't blame him either.

'I hope you're not going to eat all of those at once!' said Granny, grinning her false teeth at me.

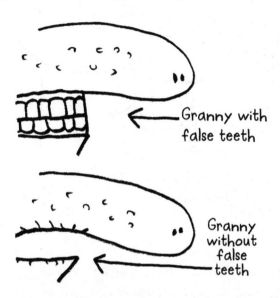

Granny with false teeth

Granny without false teeth

'What. Ever,' I said in my self-checkout robot voice, backing off from Granny and Mr Hodgepodge in **Future Ratboy** slow motion, like in the episode where he was about to be eaten by a Giant Robot Grandma.

I caught up with Bunky outside and was just about to say, 'Salute. Your. Brilliant. And. Amazing. Leader,' in my self-checkout robot voice when I saw something horrible.

Sitting outside the coffee shop on the corner, playing on his phone and sipping on a can of Fronkle, was Professor Smugly, except this wasn't a dream so it was just plain old Gordon Smugly.

'Gordon!' said Bunky, spitting chunks of Cola Flavour Not Bird everywhere.

'Ah, my fellow **Future Ratboy** expert!' said Gordon, smugly. He was wearing a new pair of the **Future Ratboy** trainers I'd been asking my mum for for a million years.

self-lacing

don't know what this bit does, but looks keel

'I wanted to talk to you, Bunky,' he said, over the top of his phone. 'It's about . . .' He stopped speaking and looked at me. 'Barry, do you mind?' he said, putting the phone down on the chair next to him.

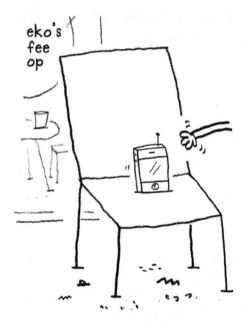

eko's
fee
op

There were three chairs, and now only one of them was empty.

'Whatev,' I said, which is short for 'whatever', and I went and sat on the edge of the pavement with my shoes in the gutter, hoping that my feet would get run over by a car because I've always wondered how much it'd hurt, plus if they did get run over I could blame Gordon Smugly.

The sun was going down in the sky and from where I was sitting it was the same size as a Cola Flavour Not Bird. I held one of the sweets up against the sun and it glowed like a giant cola-flavoured star.

'Screech!' parked a car, missing my feet by a billimetre, and in its reflection I could see Bunky and Gordon Smugly talking and laughing.

'Bunky! Salute!' I shouted, holding up my glowing Not Bird.

'Not now, Barry,' said Bunky, and
Gordon shook his head like a mum
would about her annoying child.

After the time it takes to watch
about three episodes of **Future Ratboy**,
me and Bunky left.

'What in the world of unkeelness was that about?' I said, happy to be getting away.

'We're having a sleepover round his on Friday night,' said Bunky, flying a Cola Flavour Not Bird into his mouth.

'Salute,' I said, even though I wasn't sure if I was invited.

The Poo Chair

Unsuddenly it was Monday, which I haven't got round to shortening yet, but when I do I'm thinking of calling it 'M'.

Bunky and me managed to dodge Mr Hodgepodge and Granny's morning kiss, and getting a lift to school, which was good because I hadn't been into Three Thumb Rita's for a while and was worried she'd think I didn't like her any more because of her third thumb.

boiled-sweet door handle (keel times a million)

third
thumb

'Barry Loser, my number-one
customer!' she said as I came through
the door playing it keel times ten.
'I haven't seen you for a few days.'

'That's cos he's found a new favourite sweet!' said Bunky, pulling out a packet of Feeko's Cola Flavour Not Birds and holding it up to her face.

'NOT!' I said quickly, going over to the Thumb Sweets. I didn't get my usual excited feeling looking at them, but I bought three packets anyway.

I opened one and poked a thumb into my mouth. 'Mmmmmm, I love the nail bit,' I said, and I used my tongue to slot it into the hole where one of my teeth had fallen out the week before. 'Look, I've got a thumb growing out of my gums!' I said.

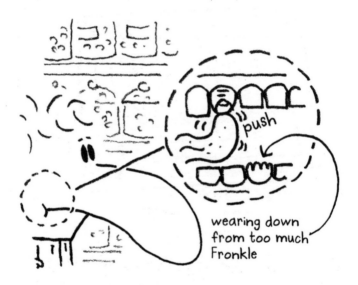

push

wearing down from too much Fronkle

'How's your granny?' said Rita,
because they went to school together
a million years ago. Granny has a
photo of them when they were my
age, but I don't believe it's real.

seaweed

'Wrinkly,' I said, and Bunky snortled.
After that we completely ran out of
things to say, so me and Bunky left.

I put the Thumb Sweets in my
rucksack and ate Cola Flavour
Not Birds for the whole morning at
school, sneaking them into my mouth
every time Mr Hodgepodge looked
away, which was constantly, because
he's always staring at his photo of
Granny Harumpadunk.

Scared
Flavour
Not Bird

Then it was lunchtime, even though I wasn't hungry because I'd eaten nine million Not Birds.

I didn't have a packed lunch because my dad had forgotten to do the shopping, which had got him into trouble with my mum, so I joined the queue in the canteen with Bunky, who's an expert at school dinners.

'Make sure you get a good glass,' said Bunky, taking one off the top of a stack and turning it upside down to look at the bottom. 'Yes, a three!' he said, holding it up to my face. I used my **Future Ratboy** super-rat-vision eyes to zoom in and saw the tiniest little three in the world, written on the bottom of the glass.

clink

I grabbed one and turned it upside down. 'Ha, ha! Nine hundred and ninety-nine!' I laughed, holding it up next to my face and smiling like I was in an advert for a scratched-up old glass.

'Ooh, bad luck, Loser,' said a smelly voice behind my shoulder and it echoed in the empty glass and went up my earhole and into my nose.

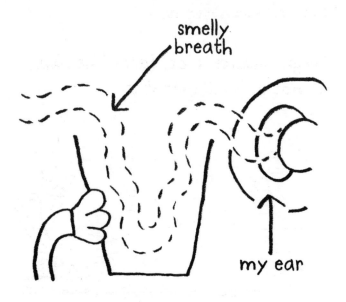

smelly breath

my ear

Gordon Smugly had joined the queue and was reaching over me to grab a glass off the stack.

'I don't think he understands this game,' I whispered into Bunky's ear, and a bit of chewed-up Cola Flavour Not Bird flew into it.

'Arrgh, thanks a lot, Barry,' he said, but not as if he meant it.

'Number one, naturally!' said Gordon, holding his glass up, and from everybody's jealous faces I realised that maybe nine hundred and ninety-nine wasn't such a good number after all.

'That means I get to choose who I sit next to,' said Gordon once we'd got our food. 'Bunky, would you care to join me?'

'Who gets The Poo Chair?' said Darren, farting and burping his way up to the table with his can of Fronkle and chips.

'That would be our friend Mr Loser, I believe,' said Gordon. 'Unless someone got an even rubbisher number?'

So that was how Bunky ended up sitting next to Gordon at the top of the table, with me at the end on the only chair that has a cushiony seat, which was actually quite comfy thank you very much indeed amen.

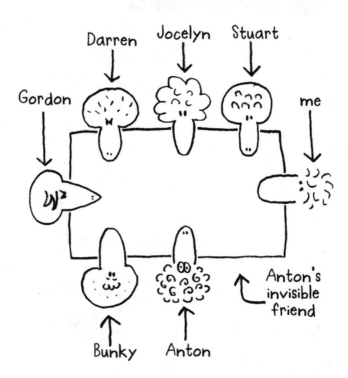

Darren

Jocelyn

Stuart

Gordon

me

Bunky

Anton

Anton's invisible friend

Barold Loser

What I didn't realise about the cushiony chair is that it's the oldest, most farted-into chair in the whole school, and that includes Mr Hodgepodge's.

x 1,000

poo molecule

x 1,000,000

At first I was quite enjoying sitting on it, and I did a little blowoff to celebrate, feeling it seep into the fabric.

Then as I got more comfortable and the cushion bit heated up from my bum being on it, I noticed a disgusting smell seeping up from between my legs, and it wasn't my blowoff.

'Poooo-weeee, Barry, you're getting more like your Grandpa Hodgepodge every day,' said Anton Mildew, who was sitting two seats away from me with a gap in-between us. There's always a gap next to Anton because of his invisible friend.

Anton's invisible friend

'Ah, the cushion awakes!' said Gordon, leaning forwards. He sliced a pea in half and pushed it on to his fork next to a Cola-Flavour-Not-Bird-sized piece of potato.

He brought the mouthful up to the hole in the middle of his face and slotted it in, then changed his mind and took it out again.

'Looks like The Poo Chair has found its rightful owner!' he snortled to himself, and everyone else laughed, but not like they thought it was that funny.

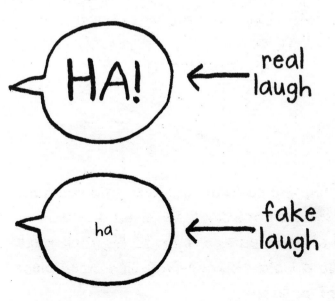

'Whaaat-evvvv,' I said, which is LONG for 'Whatev'.

'You're quite the one for shortening words, aren't you, Barry?' said Gordon, putting the food into his mouth and taking it out again.

'What's that, Gordo?' I said, which is short for Gordon, and Anton Mildew did a snortle, nudging his invisible friend.

'I wonder what BARRY's short for. If HARRY is short for HAROLD . . .' said Gordon, and he put the food back in his mouth and stopped, like when you pause someone ugly on a DVD.

'It's short for KEEL,' I said, and I did a smile like I was in an advert for how keel I was.

How Keel is Barry Loser

ROAR

'I was thinking something more like BAROLD,' said Gordon, and he bit the food off his fork. 'Yes, Barold Loser. That suits you just fine,' he said, and everyone at the table laughed, Bunky included.

The walk of loser- ness

For the whole rest of the week, every time Mr Hodgepodge called me Barry, Gordon Smugly shouted, 'Barold!' and everyone laughed, Mr Hodgepodge included.

Then it was Fri, which I'd sort of been dreading, seeing as I was sleeping over at Gordon's, even though I wasn't sure if I was invited.

I felt like a bit of a loser, walking to his house after school behind Bunky, with my **Future Ratboy** sleeping bag and fully packed rucksack, which I'd hidden my cuddly Not Bird in.

I'd made sure it was switched off, because I didn't want it saying 'NOT' after everything everyone said, which is what it does when it's turned on.

Halfway down Gordon's road, I spotted an empty packet of Cola Flavour Not Birds, sitting in the gutter like a plastic leaf.

'Salute!' I shouted to Bunky.

'Could you perhaps stop making me salute things all the while?' said Bunky, trying to sound like Gordon.

'Sorr-rry,' I said, doing a mini-twirl-
salute to the packet and running
to catch up.

'I don't think Gordon invited you by
the way,' said Bunky as he pressed the
doorbell, and the noise of the buzzer
made all the little hairs on my body
stand up on end.

'Oh no, not HIM,' Gordon Smugly's voice said from behind the door. He opened it and smiled at Bunky. 'Do come in,' he said, and we walked into his house, me last.

Mr & Mrs Smugly

Gordon's house was so big that you could probably fit my whole one inside his kitchen.

'Mama, Papa, this is Bunky, the one I told you about,' said Gordon to his mum and dad, and I looked at Bunky to see if he wanted to do a snortle about the Mama-Papa bit but he was too busy smiling all smugly to notice.

'I'm sure it is,' said Mrs Smugly, who was rushing around getting ready to go out.

She was wearing a necklace made out of wooden beads the size of mini scotch eggs.

'Don't forget to feed Spencer,' said
Mr Smugly, and I imagined Gordon
spoon-feeding their butler, putting the
food into his mouth and taking it out
before he could take a bite. Then I saw
a cat bowl with Spencer written on it.

'We're just next door if anything terrible happens,' said Mrs Smugly, and she kissed Gordon on his horrible cheek, leaving a massive bright-red lipstick mark on it.

no bit of wall for me to lean on

'Don't do anything I wouldn't do!' said Mr Smugly, and he kissed Gordon right where the lipstick mark was, which made his lips go red like he'd put make-up on for his night out.

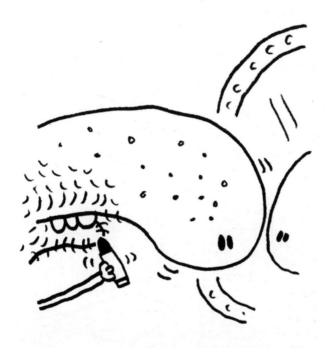

The front door slammed and Mr and Mrs Smugly were gone.

'Can of Fronkle, Bunky?' said Gordon, opening the fridge, which was completely full of all the keelest stuff, unlike mine, since my mum and dad were still arguing over whose turn it was to go shopping.

He poured the can into a glass and got some ice cubes out of the freezer and plopped a couple into the drink.

'Here you go, Bunky,' he said, passing him the glass in front of my nose.

'Can I have an ice cube?' I said, because my mum always tells me to ask for water instead of Fronkle when I'm at someone's house, and ice cubes are just frozen water.

'No, I don't think so,' said Gordon, and he put them back in the freezer.

'Where's your toilet?' I asked, because I needed a wee, but also to get away from Gordon for a bit.

'Follow your nose,' said Gordon, so I followed my nose, which found the toilet really easily, thank you very much amen.

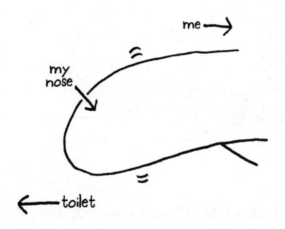

me ———→

my
nose

←——— toilet

Nosey-poos

'You're my friend, aren't you,
Noseypoos,' I said into the bathroom
mirror to cheer myself up, but it didn't
work because I could hear Gordon and
Bunky outside the door, giggling.

'Having fun with Noseypoos?' said Gordon when I came out, but that wasn't what bothered me. He had my rucksack, and it was open.

'I can't believe you brought THIS!' said Bunky. He was holding my cuddly Not Bird up in one hand and the glass of Fronkle in the other. 'Let's turn it on,' he said, and started fiddling around and spilling Fronkle all over it.

'Give it back, Bunky,' I said, and for a
millisecond I saw him do his guilty face,
then Gordon grabbed the Not Bird and
turned it on.

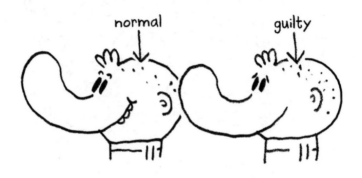

normal   guilty

'Barry LOSER is keel,' said Gordon,
holding the Not Bird up to my face.

'NOT!' it screeched.

'Barry Loser is keel!' said Bunky, because he's too stupid to think of anything himself.

'NOT!' screeched Not Bird again.

'I invited Barry LOSER to my house,' said Gordon, and him and Bunky joined in with Not Bird, shouting, 'NNNNOOOOOOTTTTTTT!'

I grabbed Not Bird and my rucksack and walked to the front door at **Future Ratboy** trying-not-to-cry speed and fiddled with the lock, trying to open it.

'There's a knack,' said Gordon, and he reached over and opened it really easily. 'I believe this is yours,' he said, passing me my **Future Ratboy** sleeping bag.

I tried to stuff it into my rucksack with my Not Bird and all my stupid Thumb Sweets, and the torch I'd packed in case we were going to have a midnight feast, but it wouldn't fit, so I put it under my arm and walked home, with Noseypoos as my only friend.

Rubbishest Sat ever

Because that day had been a Fri, the next one was a Sat, so I woke up half expecting to find Bunky sitting downstairs watching TV as per usual, even though I knew he would still be at Gordon's.

What I completely and utterly DIDN'T
expect to find sitting in the living room
was Bunky's mum in her pink
tracksuit and glow-in-the-dark
yellow leg warmers.

'Ooh, hello Barry, I thought you'd be
out with Bunky and Gordon,' she said,
stretching her leg on the coffee table.

'If you're not doing anything you can help me with the shopping,' my mum said, giving my dad an evil stare through the window. After that I watched from the garden with him as my mum and Mrs Bunky did their dance workout.

stretch

They'd found a video on the internet of some woman in her front room dancing around and shouting like she thought she was an actual instructor.

In one bit her cat walked into the room and she accidentally trod on it, which made me and my dad laugh, even though we weren't really enjoying our Sats all that much.

Mother's Day present from me

Feeko's chocolate digestive

Keelest mum ever

When Bunky's mum had gone and my mum had had her cup of tea and a biscuit, we drove to Feeko's Supermarket, which is probably the most boring sentence I've ever said.

I didn't enjoy Feeko's this time, walking behind my mum, who has to go through the whole clothes department in slow motion before you even get to the actual shopping bit.

'That's nice isn't it – two forty-nine,' she was saying, holding up a clothes hanger with something boring hanging off it, when I looked through a gap in one of the shelves and saw a scene that made me feel like I'd smashed on to the floor like a bottle of dropped ketchup.

Bunky and Gordon were at the
Cola Flavour Not Birds display, filling
up a whole basket with MY favourite
sweets. Gordon said something that I
couldn't hear, then shouted 'NOT!' and
Bunky cracked up and saluted him with
his twirly-hand-salute.

hair goes off page

'Ooh look, it's Bunky,' said my mum, giving me a nudge, and I wondered if her and Bunky's mum had had a chat about why we weren't hanging out together, because there'd been a bit after their workout when they were talking all seriously and looking at me and my dad through the window.

I ignored her and kept my eyes looking down for the whole rest of the shopping so that I wouldn't see Bunky and Gordon, which was actually quite fun because they've started putting adverts on the floor in Feeko's now.

I was reading one for Feeko's Noodles where the N and S had rubbed off so it just said 'OODLE', when I looked up and realised I was on my own.

An old grandad was next to me,
counting his coins to see if he had
enough to buy a scotch egg. The coins
were in a little old falling-apart brown
envelope, and I would've felt a bit
sorry for him if he hadn't had what
looked like a million disgusting, mouldy,
half-sucked Thumb Sweets growing out
of his face and hands.

'MUUUUUUMMMMMM!' I screamed,
zigzagging down the aisles like a
runaway trolley.

I found her at the self-checkout
machine, moaning about how long
it was taking to beep everything
through by herself, and I grabbed her
leg warmer until I stopped shaking like
a Feeko's jelly, which I'd just seen an
advert on the floor for, by the way.

'You. Are. So. Un. Keel,' said a smug, ugly robot voice, and Gordon Smugly glided past like a hoverpoo.

'Hello, Barold,' said Bunky, chewing on a Cola Flavour Not Bird and giggling.

'What. Ev,' I said in my self-checkout robot voice, and carried on hugging my mum's leg.

Annoyingly, my mum was doing HER self-checkout voice all the way home from Feeko's, partly to try and cheer me up, but also because she'd picked up a leaflet for a competition to become The Voice of Feeko's Self-Checkout Machine.

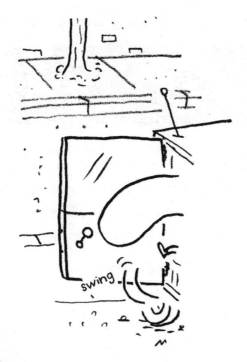

'That'll be two forty-nine,' she said, pretending be a taxi driver as I got out of the car at home. Usually I'd do a fake laugh to keep her happy, but my Sat had been so rubbish that I didn't even smile.

Zeditis

I tried to get out of going to school on Monday morning by pretending I had Zeditis, which is an illness **Future Ratboy** had in an episode of **Future Ratboy** once.

It's where you snore actual Zs like people do in cartoons, and when you wake up your whole room is full of Zs and you can't get out of bed.

'I think it's Zeditis,' I croaked from under the duvet.

'It's either that or Gordon-Smuglyitis,' said my mum, giving me a hug through the duvet, then whipping it off and tickling me until I nearly weed myself with laughter.

I was glad my mum made me go
into school in the end, because I'd
completely forgotten that
Mr Hodgepodge had organised a
trip to Mogden Museum.

'Ooh, that sounds like fun!' said
Three Thumb Rita when I popped in
to buy five more packets of Thumb
Sweets to keep her happy, even though
I'd gone off them even more since the
scotch-egg man in the supermarket
with the weird face and hands.

'Maybe it'll give you some ideas for your Halloween costume!' she said, and I looked at her and thought about how she looked a bit like a witch, except a nice one.

Ghost Barry

Frankenbarry's Monster

Count Barrycula

The Hunchbarry of Notre Dame

I'd been trying to work out what to wear for Halloween for a while, seeing as it was at the end of the week, but now I didn't have any friends there didn't seem much point.

'Have fun!' said Rita as I walked out, and she gave me a double thumbs up, apart from it was a triple, because of her extra thumb.

Regular Barry

Playing it oodle

While I'm talking about thumbs, what's weird is that I had a **Future Ratboy** plaster on the one on my left hand. My mum stuck it on to make me feel better about Bunky and Gordon, which sounds a bit stupid but it actually worked.

Future
Ratboy
plasters

five designs!

Ouchville
NOT!

x20

Unkeel

'A Future Ratman sticking plaster? What will they think of next!' said Granny's voice out of nowhere. Then I realised it'd come out of her wrinkly old body, which was standing next to the coach that everyone was getting into to go to the museum.

'What in the name of oodle are you doing here?' I said, replacing the word 'keel' with 'oodle' because after hearing Gordon say 'keel' in Feeko's on Sat I'd realised it was completely un-oodle.

'I invited her!' said Mr Hodgepodge, leaning his face on Granny's shoulder so that she looked like a two-headed Granny Harumpadunk.

'Oh, well that's just OODLE,' I said, and got on to the coach.

The first two faces I saw the moment I got inside were Bunky's and Gordon's. They were sitting next to each other, playing on Gordon's phone like a two-headed Gordon Smugly.

'Morning, Barold,' said Gordon, and Bunky looked up from the phone and snortled.

'Oh, is it morning?' I said, looking around as if I hadn't realised. 'Thanks for clearing that up for me, Gordon, I was just about to have my dinner and go to beddypoos.'

'What, with your cuddly Not Bird?' said Gordon, and Bunky snortled again, even though I know he sleeps with a bit of old blanket called Mr Ponkles.

I walked past them, making sure Bunky
saw my thumb-in-plaster so that he'd
feel sorry for me, and headed to
the back of the coach where
Darren Darrenofski was sitting.

'Barry! Come and sit next to me!'
burped Darren, doing a blowoff at
the same time.

Anton Mildew and his invisible friend were in the seats in front of me and Darren, so we spent most of the trip scraping the back of Anton's neck with Darren's ruler.

'You won't like Invis when he's angry,' said Anton through the gap between the seats, his face all squidged like it was stuck between lift doors.

'I don't like him FULL STOP,' said Darren, and he drew a full stop on Anton's forehead with a blue felt-tip pen.

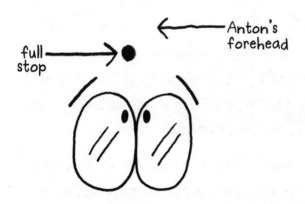

full stop

Anton's forehead

Benjamin Bottle

I don't know why we bothered getting the coach at all, because Mogden Museum is only a ten-minute walk from school, so we got there in about three seconds.

As I walked through the car park to the museum, a bit of gravel got stuck on the bottom of my shoe and started scraping every time I put my foot down, which was about once every half a second.

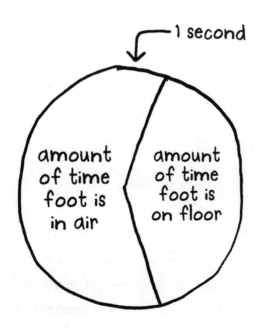

1 second

amount of time foot is in air

amount of time foot is on floor

'Scrape,' said Darren, every time I did a scrape. It was really annoying, but also made me do a snortle, which was nice because I hadn't been doing that many snortles since I'd stopped hanging out with Bunky.

146

'Snortle, snortle,' said a voice that sounded like Gordon's. I turned round and it was Gordon, not that I was surprised, because the voice really had sounded exactly like his. 'Let me guess, something's happened that's the FUNNIEST THING IN THE WHOLE WIDE WORLD AMEN,' he said, now sounding more like me than himself.

'Yeah, I just remembered your cat's called Spencer,' I said, scraping along.

first ever scrape in history of universe

'What's that, SCRAPE NUMBER TWO HUNDRED MILLION IN THE HISTORY OF THE UNIVERSE?' Gordon shouted, and I felt like a loser because that's the sort of oodle thing I'd say, except all of a sudden it sounded really un-oodle.

'Yeah, why don't you do a salute to your shoe or something!' said Bunky, and I was about to give him a super-reverse-twizzle-salute when the door to the museum creaked open and we all did a massive gasp.

We were gasping because inside the door stood the shortest, fattest dinosaur any of us had ever seen, especially as none of us had ever seen one in real life before.

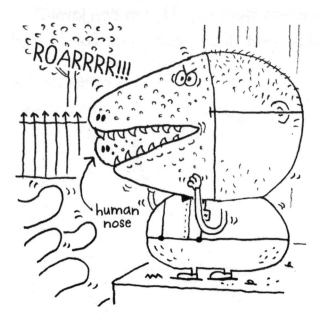

'Roooaaarrrr!' it said, and we all hid behind Mr Hodgepodge, who was hiding behind Granny Harumpadunk.

'I want my Mr Ponkles!' screamed Bunky, and I snortled to myself because by now I'd realised that dinosaurs don't wear baggy old trousers and have badges on their jumpers that say 'Hi, I'm Benjamin Bottle and I'll be your guide for today!'

The dinosaur took off his mask and we all gasped again, because underneath was the biggest nose ever in the history of noses amen.

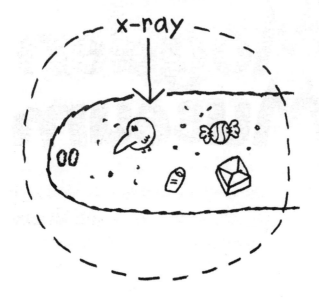

'Hi, I'm Benjamin Bottle and I'll be your guide for today!' said the dinosaur-man, and his voice was so oodle, it was as if his nose had sweets inside instead of bogies.

Mogden
Museum

'Hello, Hodge!' said Benjamin Bottle, high fiving Mr Hodgepodge, who completely missed because he's got cross-eyes.

'Benjy!' said Mr Hodgepodge, thinking he was all oodle because he had a friend. 'Kids, this is my friend Benjamin Bottle,' he said as we walked in, and we all rolled our eyes because we'd already worked that out.

rolling eyes

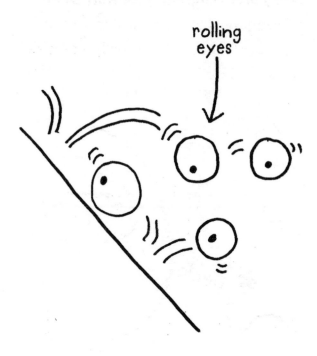

'Today we're going to learn about Mogden's ancient history, starting with the dinosaurs!' said Benjamin Bottle as we walked into the first room.

'Sounds like a trip down memory lane for you, Mr Hodgepodge,' said Gordon, and everyone laughed. I looked over at Mr Hodgepodge and saw Granny Harumpadunk give him a little peck on the cheek.

peck

dinosaur

Darren

'Who can tell me the name of this one?' asked Benjamin Bottle, pointing at a dinosaur skeleton in the middle of the room that looked exactly like Darren Darrenofski except without his skin on.

'Darren Darrensaurus?' I said, excited because it was so funny.

'Barrylosersaurus Rex more like!' said Bunky, copying my joke, and everyone laughed.

Losersaurus

sabre-toothed dog poo

'Now now, children, this is serious stuff,' said Mr Hodgepodge, and I felt sorry for him because he'd planned this whole trip and no one was taking it seriously. 'Just imagine, these creatures were roaming Mogden millions of years ago!' he said, doing an impression of a dinosaur walking around with cross-eyes.

'Did they still have a Feeko's Supermarket back then?' asked Anton Mildew, looking up at the dinosaur's hands. He was probably imagining it carrying a shopping bag home with his dinner in it or something.

tonight's dinner: woolly mammoth bolognese

Feeko's

'No, Anton, they did not have a Feeko's,' said Mr Hodgepodge. 'The whole of Mogden would have been a swamp,' he said, then he added, 'Or something,' and looked over at Benjamin Bottle because he didn't really know what he was talking about.

Your new Feeko's superstore will be here in 65 million years!

'Yes that's right, Hodge, Mogden was one big swamp for millions of years,' said Benjamin Bottle, shuffling off into the next room, which was empty apart from a big glass box in the middle.

'The swamp was where this man lived - and died . . .' he said, nodding his head towards the box.

I ran up to the glass and peered through, and I almost did a scream like the time in Feeko's when I bumped into the old grandad with the Thumb Sweets growing out of his face.

gasp

Mogden Man

Lying down on a bit of fake plastic mud was a completely shrivelled-up old man, his mouth wide open so that you could see his teeth, which were yellow like the bits of corn on the cob you get in dog poos. His eyes were open too, but there was nothing inside the holes.

'This is Mogden Man,' whispered Benjamin Bottle, crouching down so that he was our height, even though he's only about a centimetre taller anyway.

'But what happened to him?' asked Anton, hiding behind his invisible friend.

'Nobody knows how he died,' whispered Benjamin Bottle, 'just that the swamp kept his body preserved for thousands of years, like a jar of Feeko's pickled onions . . .'

'Ooh, pickled onions! I could just have one now!' said Granny Harumpadunk, who was on the other side of the glass box. It looked like she was inside it, which wouldn't have surprised me, what with how wrinkly she is.

'I'd sack whoever cleans this place,' said Gordon Smugly, signing his stupid name in the dust on the glass box.

I rolled my eyes, because it felt a bit stupid to be talking about dust when there's a million-year-old dead man lying there with his mouth wide open, and Benjamin Bottle gave me a wink, and we headed off into the next room.

Thingy-majigs

Instead of being empty with one glass box in the middle, this room was empty with glass boxes all the way round the edge. Inside the boxes were millions of those things I can never remember the name of, all different colours and sizes.

'What's all this craziness about?' said
Gordon, reminding me of Professor
Smugly from my nightmare, and I
wondered if the museum had any glass
boxes with hoverpoos in them.

'Caterpillars!' shouted Benjamin Bottle, going right up to Gordon's face so their noses were touching. 'They love a swamp. Mogden used to be teeming with them!'

'And no, they didn't go to Feeko's, Anton,' said Mr Hodgepodge. 'Although I did see one in the garden last week.'

'Oh yes, they're still around. Big pink squidgy one bit me just the other day,' whispered Benjamin Bottle, winking at me. His face was still right up against Gordon's. 'Chomp!' he shouted, holding his hand up.

He'd bent his little finger over, but from where Gordon was standing it looked like it'd been bitten off.

I thought of Three Thumb Rita and how Benjamin Bottle was a bit like her, except he was a man, and had ten fingers instead of eleven, even though he was pretending he had nine right now.

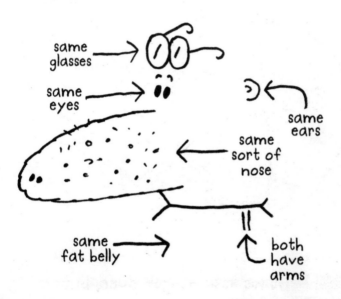

same glasses

same eyes

same ears

same sort of nose

same fat belly

both have arms

'That couldn't happen!' said Gordon, but not smugly, more scaredly, and it made me come up with one of my brilliant and amazing ideas.

'Oh yes it could!' I shouted, holding up my **Future Ratboy** thumb-in-plaster. 'A thingymajig bit ME yesterday and my THUMB fell off! I had to stick it back on with a plaster!'

'Did you get your cuddly Not Bird to kiss it better?' said Gordon, gliding over like a hoverpoo, but one that's still a bit scared. He looked at my plaster and his eyebrows went up about fifteen centimetres. 'Er, Barold, what in the name of keelness are you doing wearing a **Future Ratboy** plaster when Bunky and I are his number-one fans?' he shouted.

'This!' I said, and I Future-Ratboy-plastered his stupid mouth shut.

White chocolate Not Bird moon

I don't think Gordon believed me about my thumb falling off, but it felt good to make him look like a loser, even though he ripped the plaster off straight away.

After that, we went into about three hundred more rooms and by the end of the trip I'd seen so many keel things, nothing could shock me any more.

That was until I started walking home on my own after the coach had dropped us back at school. It was pitch black apart from the moon, which was hanging in the sky like an enormous white chocolate Not Bird with a chunk bitten out of it.

'Don't worry Noseypoos, we'll be home soon,' I was saying as I scraped along with the bit of gravel in my shoe, when I felt a tap on my shoulder. 'DON'T KILL ME!' I screamed, turning round, thinking it was Mogden Man, but no one was there.

Then I looked three centimetres to the left and saw Anton Mildew, who still had the blue full stop on his forehead, by the way.

'I won't, but Invis might,' he said,
looking a bit scared himself. 'He's still
angry at you from the coach.'

Invis

'Sorry, Invis,' I said, and we walked
back to my house. 'Mum, Dad, this is
Anton and Invis,' I said when we got
inside. 'Can they stay for dinner?'

'As long as they like scotch eggs,' said my mum, because that's all we had left in the fridge since her and my dad were STILL arguing about whose turn it was to do the shopping.

'Our favourite!' said Anton, putting his arm round Invis, and I rolled my eyes to my mum like mums do to each other.

It was quite oodle hanging out with Anton and Invis, because they're really easy to boss around. 'Salute how oodle my room is,' I said when we went upstairs, and they both immediately saluted, although not as well as Bunky used to.

At eight o'clock Anton's mum phoned up, crying about where he was, so my dad drove him and Invis home.

'See you both tomorrow!' I shouted as they drove off, even though you can't see Invis because he's invisible.

Mr Scrapey-foot McLoser

The next day at school, everyone except for me was getting excited about what they were wearing to go trick-or-treating for Halloween, which was on Fri.

'Gordon's got a brand new
Future Ratboy outfit!' Bunky was
saying as me and my new best friends,
Anton and Invis, walked past in the
playground at lunch.

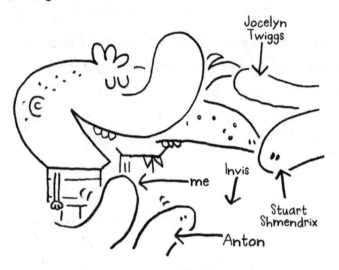

'And Bunky's going as Not Bird!' said
Gordon, and I rolled my eyes like mums
do to themselves, because me and
Bunky used to go trick-or-treating as
Future Ratboy and Not Bird.

'What are you going as, Mr Scrapey-foot McLoser?' Gordon shouted at me, because I still hadn't taken the bit of gravel out of my shoe yet.

'I'm dressing up as your mum,' I shouted back, and I thought about how that actually wasn't a bad idea, seeing as I could make her necklace out of scotch eggs.

'Do you wanna come trick-or-treating with me and Invis?' asked Anton as we walked off, me all scrapily. 'He's going as an invisible dinosaur!'

'Whatev,' I said, which was short for 'Yes, definitely.'

Invisisaurus
Rex

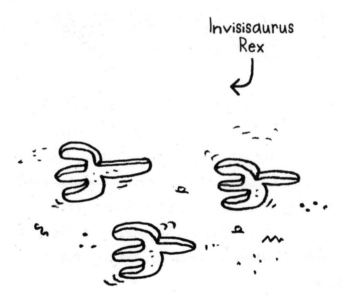

Three Thumb Barry

In Drama on Weds I tried to make Bunky feel bad for going off with Gordon by dressing up as Three Thumb Rita. I put an old mop on my head and stuffed the Poo Chair cushion up my jumper and stuck one of my million spare Thumb Sweets on to my right hand.

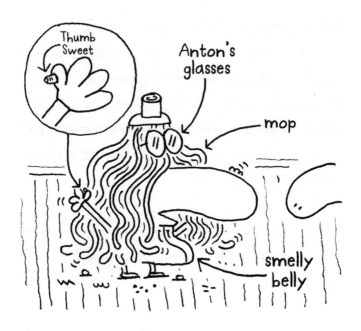

'Ooh, hello Barry, I haven't seen you
for a while,' I said, as Anton pretended
to walk into my shop. He was playing
me, except he didn't look as oodle.
'Where's your best friend, Blinky?
Bonky?'

'I don't know, Rita, he's . . . he's disappeared,' said Anton, looking down, sadly. I was quite impressed with how he said it, seeing as I'd only just given him the lines. 'I see you have adverts on your floor now,' he said. 'What's that "Smuglies" one for?'

'Smuglies are my newest sweets,' I said, pretending to pass him a packet. 'They're much better than my old ones!'

packet of
Smuglies

'But I've been eating the old ones my whole life,' said Anton. 'Should I really leave them and go off with some new sweet that I don't even know?'

'GOOD POINT, BARRY, NO YOU SHOULDN'T,' I said loudly and clearly towards where Bunky was sitting, 'YOU SHOULD CARRY ON HANGING OUT WITH YOUR OLD FAVOURITE SWEETS.'

I looked over but he was playing on Gordon's phone and chewing on a Cola Flavour Not Bird.

'Very interesting,' said Mr Hodgepodge, giving me a funny look, which wasn't surprising seeing as I had a mop on my head. 'What do you think, class?'

'I think Barold might be going a bit mad!' said Gordon, and everyone laughed.

Million Thumbs Barry

I kept my eyes looking down for the whole rest of the week so that I didn't see Gordon and Bunky, who were always walking around together, saying 'keel' and doing salutes.

'I'm sorry, love,' said my mum, passing me a toffee apple and giving me a little cuddle. It was Halloween night and I was dressed as the scotch egg man from Feeko's, with all my old Thumb Sweets stuck all over my face and hands. My dad was in the garden barbecuing sausages because he'd finally given in and gone shopping.

The doorbell rang and Mrs Mildew came in with Anton and Invis. Anton was dressed completely as himself, apart from the faded blue felt-tip full stop on his forehead.

'Haven't we met before?' said my mum, passing Mrs Mildew a toffee apple but not giving her a cuddle. 'There's something very familiar about you.'

'No, I don't think so,' said Mrs Mildew, and my dad's face appeared at the window with a sausage next to it.

'The dance workout lady!' he mouthed, waggling the sausage around.

I looked up at Mrs Mildew, and started laughing for what felt like the first time in ages, because she was the dance workout lady from the internet that'd trodden on her cat.

'Oh, Timothy is fine, just a bit of a limp,' she said when I asked how the cat was, and I wondered why everyone at my school gave their cats human names.

After that we all had burnt sausages together and I drew a million more blue felt-tip-pen full stops on to Anton's face and sellotaped eyebrow-sausages on to his glasses, and we headed out to go trick-or-treating.

The scary doorbell

We'd trick-or-treated nine billion roads and collected six trillion sweets each when we turned a corner and I realised we were on Granny's street.

'Let's trick-or-treat Granny Harumpadunk!' I said, and we ran up to her house and rang the bell. It's a musical doorbell, and she'd set it to Spooky, so it was a bit scary, standing there waiting for her to answer with it going 'wooooooooooooh' like the ghost of a dead doorbell.

WOOOOOOOH

We stood there for the length of the **Future Ratboy** Halloween Special, but nobody answered the door.

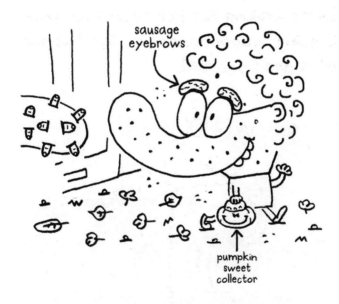

sausage eyebrows

pumpkin sweet collector

'Maybe she's dead?' said Anton, shrugging his arms as if he thought she probably was and we should move on to another house for more sweets.

A rocket screeched out of the little
park at the end of Granny's road and
exploded in the sky like an enormous
glow-in-the-dark blowoff. 'Fireworks!' I
shouted, and we ran towards them.

Peering through the bushes, you could just make out a group of people standing around a big fire, nattering. One of them was lighting the rockets, and the whole crowd ooohed every time there was a bang.

I used my **Future Ratboy**
super-rat-vision eyes and zoomed
in on the rocket-lighterer and did a
massive gasp.

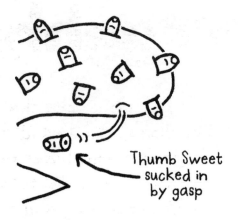

Thumb Sweet
sucked in
by gasp

I was gasping because it was
Benjamin Bottle, and the crowd were
Mr Hodgepodge, Granny Harumpadunk,
her friends Ethel and Doreen, and
Three Thumb Rita.

Ooooohs and Arrrgghhs

'Don't mind if I do,' said a voice that sounded like Gordon's, and a hand that looked like Gordon's reached over my shoulder and grabbed about thirteen of my sweets. I turned round and it was Gordon, not that I was surprised, because the voice and hand had sounded and looked exactly like his.

'What in the name of playing-it-unkeel-times-ten is going on here?' he said, chomping on my sweets. He was dressed as **Future Ratboy** and Bunky was behind him in a rubbish homemade Not Bird costume.

Bunky's Not Bird nose

RG

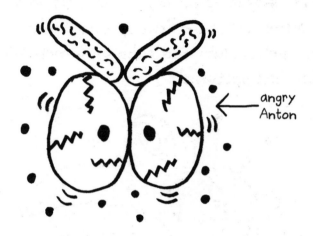

angry
Anton

'Nobody steals mine and Invis's new best friend's sweets,' said Anton, holding Invis back from punching Gordon in the face, and Gordon's face lit up like a glowing Cola Flavour Not Bird.

'Firework!' shouted Bunky, and I turned and saw a rocket coming right for us.

The crowd's 'Ooooohs!' turned into 'Arrrgghhs!' as the rocket burst through the bushes and zoomed past us, exploding on the other side of the street.

'ARRRGGGHHHHH, IT GOT MEEEEE!!!'
screamed Gordon, and for a second I
forgot I hated him. Then I remembered
that I hated him again, because the
rocket hadn't got him at all. It hadn't
even touched him. 'MY FACE!!!' he
screamed, kicking Anton's sweets on to
the pavement and running off, giggling.

'MY SWEETS!' shouted Anton, scrabbling around to pick them up. I stared at Bunky, and for a billisecond he smiled at me like when we were friends, then he turned and ran after Gordon.

'Forget the sweets!' I whisper-shouted to Anton, but only because they were his, and we zigzagged off like runaway shopping trolleys.

Scrapey shoe marks

'You're back early!' said my mum when we got home, sweating and panting and giggling because it'd actually been quite exciting, running home like we were being chased by Mogden Man.

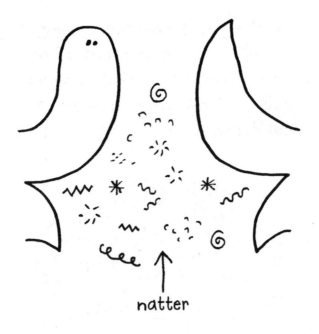

natter

Mrs Mildew was still there, nattering
to my mum about the Voice of Feeko's
Self-Checkout Machine competition,
but after that they completely ran
out of things to say so her, Anton and
Invis left and I went upstairs to eat my
sweets.

I was looking in the mirror, holding a marshmallow ear up in front of my real one, when the doorbell rang all normally, because we don't have a musical doorbell.

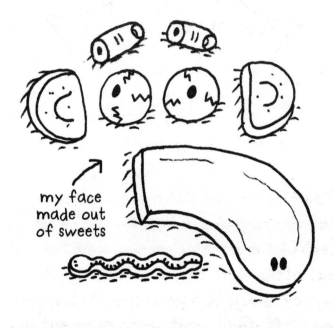

my face made out of sweets

'BAAARRR-RRYYYY!' shouted my mum up the stairs.

'WHHHHAAAATTT?' I shouted back, but it came out as 'WOHHHHH?' because my mouth was full of sweets. I poked my head out of my room and immediately knew something was wrong.

In the hallway stood Mr Hodgepodge, Benjamin Bottle, Granny Harumpadunk, Ethel, Doreen and Three Thumb Rita. They looked like a group of trick-or-treaters dressed up as a six-headed grandmonster.

'Oh, thank goodness you're all right,'
said Granny as I walked down the
stairs, trying to play it oodle.

Ethel was crying, and Doreen was
licking on a toffee apple. I wasn't
exactly sure why they were in my
hallway but I had a pretty good idea.

'What were you thinking, pretending you'd been hit by a rocket like that?' shouted Mr Hodgepodge. I could see his eyes half looking at the cold burnt sausages on the table.

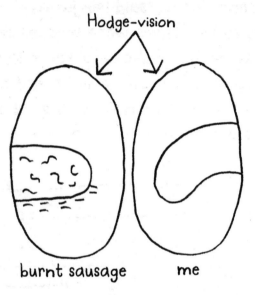

Hodge-vision

burnt sausage   me

'We thought it'd killed someone,' he carried on, but it came out all muffled because he'd reached over and stuffed a sausage in his mouth.

'It wasn't me!' I said, but I was giggling because I always giggle when I'm in trouble.

'I'm afraid your shoe says something different, Barry,' said Benjamin Bottle, sadly. 'There were scrapes on the pavement all the way from the park to here,' he said, and I rolled my eyes to myself for not getting rid of the bit of gravel.

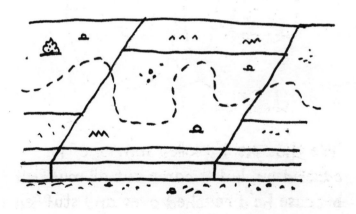

'It was Gordon. And I can prove it!' I shouted, and I came up with one of my brilliant and amazing plans right there on the spot.

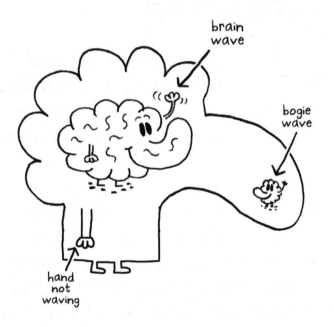

brain wave

bogie wave

hand not waving

The scream test

The next Monday morning at school, everyone was called into the assembly hall. Nobody knew what was going on except for me and Anton, and I nudged him and we snortled.

'Ladies and gentlemen, a very serious incident occurred on Friday night, in which the people gathered on this stage had their evening completely ruined by the thoughtlessness of one of you,' said Mr Hodgepodge, looking at me.

Benjamin Bottle, Granny Harumpadunk,
Ethel, Doreen and Three Thumb Rita
stood in a line behind him like they
were about to be awarded medals.

Well done
for being
so old.

I glanced over at Gordon and Bunky,
and I snortled to myself because they
looked like how I felt that night round
Gordon's house when they were being
horrible.

'I'd like Barry Loser, Anton Mildew, Gordon Smugly and Bunky to come up here please,' said Mr Hodgepodge, and we all went up on stage, Anton whispering to Invis to stay in his seat and keep his mouth shut.

'For the purposes of this experiment,
I am going to ask each one of
you children to scream,' said
Mr Hodgepodge, and he tapped me
on the shoulder. 'Barry, you first.'

'Ooh, Barold first, what a surprise,' said
Tracy Pilchard, and her, Donnatella
and Sharonella all started giggling, not
that it bothered me, because Gordon
was about to be found out.

three-headed
Tracy

'AAARRRRGGGGGHHHH!!!!' I screamed, and everyone in the whole assembly hall cracked up, Mr Hodgepodge not included.

Anton's scream was really high pitched, and Doreen winced, turning off her hearing aid so that she didn't even hear Bunky's, which was rubbish as per usual. Then it was Gordon's turn.

hearing aid built in to glasses

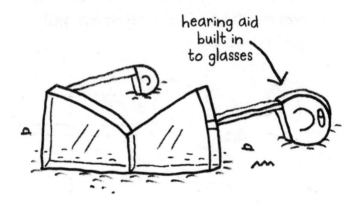

'I refuse on the grounds that I have a mild case of Zeditis,' said Gordon, smugly.

'In that case I have made my decision,' said Mr Hodgepodge, and the room went silent. 'The scream that sounded most familiar was Barry Loser's, which means he must have been the one who pretended to get hit by the firework on Halloween night,' he shouted, and everyone in the whole assembly hall gasped, me included.

← gasp

Still the scream test

'Make him run around the playground a hundred times in the nude!' screamed Tracy Pilchard, and everybody in the whole room started laughing and shouting.

I glanced over at Gordon Smugly, who was snortling and twizzle-hand-saluting himself. And that's when I came up with my EMERGENCY brilliant and amazing plan.

There was one old Thumb Sweet left at the bottom of my pocket, along with the blue felt-tip pen I'd used to draw full stops on Anton's face.

I balanced the Thumb Sweet in my palm and grabbed the pen between my thumb and finger and started drawing on to the sweet, all while still inside my pocket, by the way.

Mr Hodgepodge was murmuring with the other oldies, deciding what my punishment should be, as I shuffled my feet sideways so that I could get behind Gordon. I noticed that the bit of gravel had fallen out of my shoe and rolled my eyes to myself and did a mini-reverse-twizzle-salute in my head.

showing off

'Don't be too hard on the boy,' I heard
Benjamin Bottle whisper over all the
shouting, and I could smell his breath
as I reached over and placed the
Thumb Sweet on to Gordon's shoulder.

I'd drawn little eyes and legs on it so
that it now ever-so-slightly looked like
one of those things I can never
remember the name of.

'Children, children, please can you stop this craziness!' shouted Mr Hodgepodge to the room, but they didn't even hear him.

'What's that on Gordon's shoulder?' said Three Thumb Rita suddenly from behind us, and we all looked, Gordon included.

'AAAAARRRRRRRGGGGGGGGHHHHH!!!!!!!
CATERPILLLLAAARRRR!!!' he screamed,
exactly like he had on Halloween night
when the rocket didn't hit him, and
the whole room went silent apart
from me because I was doing a little
snortle to myself.

Plastic leaves

My snortle didn't last for long though, because after that the most ridiculous thing in the history of the universe happened.

Mr Hodgepodge decided that my scream was STILL the one that he'd heard on Halloween night, so everyone got out of trouble apart from me.

And that's how I came to be walking around the playground every lunchtime for a month with a pokey stick and a massive plastic bag picking up rubbish, which was my punishment from him.

I couldn't believe how much rubbish there was actually, once I started looking. Especially since Benjamin Bottle and Three Thumb Rita had gone into business and started selling Caterpillars, which are these new sweets in the shape of those things I can never remember the name of.

'Salute,' said a voice that sounded like Bunky's one lunchtime. I turned round and it WAS Bunky, which surprised me, seeing as I didn't think we were friends any more.

'I've got some plastic leaves for your rubbish bag,' he said, passing me a handful of empty Caterpillars packets.

'What's all this craziness about?' I said, looking for Gordon Smugly, and I saw him sitting on his own on the other side of the playground, playing on his stupid phone.

'I got bored of his games,' said Bunky, smiling. 'Plus it should be HIM collecting rubbish, not you,' he said, and he bent over to pick up a half-eaten Cola Flavour Not Bird that was floating in a puddle.

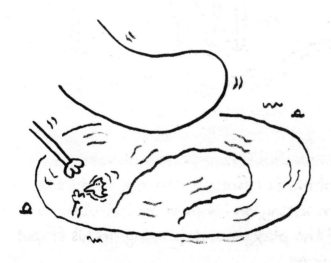

Self-checkout robot mum

It's keel being friends with Bunky again, mostly because I can say 'keel', but also because I'd forgotten how much fun we have together. Like yesterday, which was a Sat, which is my new-old favourite day, when we went to Feeko's supermarket.

'Hi Anton,' I said, missing off Invis, because he's started hanging out with Gordon these days. We were in the Ready Meals section, looking for hoverpizza, which still hasn't come out by the way.

'Can I play it oodle with Barry and Bunky?' Anton asked his mum, and I rolled my eyes to Bunky about him saying 'oodle'.

'As long as there's no screaming,' said Mrs Mildew, and she rolled her eyes to herself.

'Salute! Salute! Salute! Salute!' screamed Bunky, and I was just about to see what he was saluting when I heard something familiar behind me.

'That'll be two forty-nine,' said my mum's voice, except ever-so-slightly like a robot, and I glanced over at the self-checkout counter and collapsed to the floor like a deckchair being folded up.

cardboard
cut-out

'Let's go to Three Thumb Rita's,' I said,
and I zoomed out of Feeko's at **Future
Ratboy** speed, because there's no way
I'm spending my Sats there now that
my mum's The Voice of Feeko's.

'Oodle!' shouted Anton, running after me with Bunky, both of them blowing off with excitement, and I rolled my eyes to myself whilst doing a quadruple-reverse-twizzle-salute, which is what you do when you're keel like me.

Thend

(short for 'The End')

About the
comma putter-
innerer

Jim Smith is the keelest kids' book comma putter-innerer in the whole wide world amen.

He graduated from art school with first class honours (the best you can get) and went on to create the branding for a sweet little chain of coffee shops.

He also designs cards and gifts under the name Waldo Pancake.

Weirdly, seeing as it's about a comma putter-innerer, this whole page has only got two commas in it, I mean three.